Age 5-7

✔ KU-523-326

The Killer Cat
Strikes Back

Books by Anne Fine

A Pack of Liars
Crummy Mummy and Me
The Diary of a Killer Cat
Flour Babies
Goggle-Eyes
Jennifer's Diary
The Killer Cat Strikes Back
Loudmouth Louis
Madame Doubtfire
Notso Hotso
Only a Show
The Return of the Killer Cat
The Same Old Story Every Year
Step by Wicked Step
Stranger Danger?
The Tulip Touch
The Worst Child I Ever Had

ANNE FINE

The Killer Cat Strikes Back

Illustrated by Steve Cox

PUFFIN

PUFFIN BOOKS

Published by the Penguin Group
Penguin Books Ltd, 80 Strand, London WC2R 0RL, England
Penguin Group (USA) Inc., 375 Hudson Street, New York, New York 10014, USA
Penguin Group (Canada), 90 Eglinton Avenue East, Suite 700, Toronto, Ontario, Canada M4P 2Y3
(a division of Pearson Penguin Canada Inc.)
Penguin Ireland, 25 St Stephen's Green, Dublin 2, Ireland (a division of Penguin Books Ltd)
Penguin Group (Australia), 250 Camberwell Road, Camberwell, Victoria 3124, Australia
(a division of Pearson Australia Group Pty Ltd)
Penguin Books India Pvt Ltd, 11 Community Centre, Panchsheel Park, New Delhi – 110 017, India
Penguin Group (NZ), 67 Apollo Drive, Mairangi Bay, Auckland 1310, New Zealand
(a division of Pearson New Zealand Ltd)
Penguin Books (South Africa) (Pty) Ltd, 24 Sturdee Avenue, Rosebank, Johannesburg 2196, South Africa

Penguin Books Ltd, Registered Offices: 80 Strand, London WC2R 0RL, England

penguin.com

First published 2006
1

Text copyright © Anne Fine, 2006
Illustrations copyright © Steve Cox, 2006

The moral right of the author and illustrator has been asserted

Typeset in Baskerville by Palimpsest Book Production Ltd,
Grangemouth, Stirlingshire
Made and printed in England by Clays Ltd, St Ives plc

British Library Cataloguing in Publication Data
A CIP catalogue record for this book is available from the British Library

ISBN-13: 978-0-141-38283-8
ISBN-10: 0-141-38283-X

Contents

1: Not the best photo

OKAY, OKAY. SO stick my head in a
holly bush. I gave Ellie's mother my
mean look. It was her own fault. She
was hogging my end of the sofa. You
know – that sunny spot on the soft
cushion where I like to sit because I can
see out of the window.

Down to where the little birdy-pies
keep falling out of their nests, learning
to fly.

Yum, yum . . .

So I gave her this look. Well, she
deserved it. All I was trying to do was get
her to move along a bit so I could take

my nap. We cats need our naps. If I
don't have my nap, I get quite ratty.

So I just stood there looking at her.
That is ALL I DID.

Oh, all right. I was glowering.

But she didn't even notice. She was

2

busy flicking through the new brochure from the College of Education. 'What class shall I take?' she kept asking Ellie. 'What would suit me best? Art? Music? Great books? Dancing? Yoga?'

'Do they have classes in fixing up old

cars?' said Ellie's father. 'If they do, that's the one to take.'

He's right. That car of theirs is an embarrassment. It's a disgrace. It's just a heap of bits that rattle along the road sounding like a giant shaking rocks in a tin drum, spewing out smoke. And they will never, ever have the money to buy a new one.

The best class for Ellie's mother would be a 'Build A New Car Out Of Air' class. But I doubt if the college offers that.

I upped the glower a little – not out of nastiness, you understand. Simply to let her know I wasn't standing there admiring her beauty. My legs were *aching*.

She looked up and saw me. 'Oh, Tuffy! What a precious little crosspatch face!'

I'm like you. I hate being teased. So I just glowered some more.

Oh, all *right*. If you insist on knowing all of it, I hissed a bit.

And then I spat.

And, guess what? Suddenly she was diving into her bag and had whipped out her camera and taken a photo.

It didn't show me at my best, I must admit. I looked a little grumpy.

And you could see a bit too much of my bared teeth.

And perhaps my claws looked a shade too large and pointy. And a bit stretched out, as if I were about to lean forward and take a chunk out of someone's leg unless they shifted along the sofa a bit to let someone else on to the sunny patch.

No. Not the best photo of me.

But she seemed to like it. And it gave her an idea.

'I know!' she said. 'I'll take the art class. We do painting and pottery. But

the first thing I'm going to do is a portrait of Tuffy just like the one in the photo. Won't that be lovely?'

Oh, yes. Very lovely indeed. Lovely as *mud*.

2: Whoops!

SHE DID IT, too. Can you believe this
woman? She actually managed to get
that heap of scrap metal they park
outside our house to burst into life.
Then she drove off in it, waving, to her
first art class.

And came back with a portrait of me.

I watched from the warm spot on the
garden wall where I do a lot of my
thinking.

'Marvellous!' said the traffic warden
as Ellie's mother was pulling the
painting out of the back of the car.
'A most realistic tiger.'

'I say,' Mr Harris from next door called over the hedge as it was being carried up the path. 'I like that. Is it a poster for the new horror film they're showing in town?'

'Lovely!' said Ellie's father. 'You've captured the look perfectly.'

Ellie said nothing. I think, if I'm honest, the painting frightened her a little.

Then Ellie's mother started wondering where to put it. (Pity she

didn't ask me. I would have told her,
'How about straight in the dustbin?')

But, no. She looked around. 'What
about up on the wall in here?'

I stared.

'Yes,' she said firmly. 'It will look splendid. And everyone who visits the house can admire it.'

(Oh, yes. At their *peril*.)

But that's what she did. She found a

hook and nail, and hung her 'Portrait of Tuffy' just above the back of the sofa where everyone could admire it.

And where I could just reach it.

If I really *stretched* . . .

Whoops!

3: One little biff

OKAY, OKAY. SO clip my claws. I
scratched the cat to pieces. For pity's
sake! If anyone had the right to scratch
that painted cat's eyes out, it was me.

And it was an accident. All I did was
put out one of my sweet little paws to
give the painting one little biff. Just to
make myself feel better about it, you
could say. How could you argue it was
my fault that one of my claws caught in
the thread of the canvas?

And got *stuck*.

No one could blame me for trying to
pull my own paw free.

Over and over . . .

The picture did end up looking a bit
of a mess, I have to admit. But I felt a
whole lot better.

I sat on the wall outside and waited.
The explosion came soon enough.

'Look at this mess! My "Portrait of Tuffy" has been torn to bits!'

'It's in shreds! There are bits of painting all over the carpet!'

'Not just on the carpet! Isn't that a painted ear up on the dresser?'

'And a bit of tail hanging off that lamp?'

'I've found a paw on the window sill!' wailed Ellie.

Oh, I certainly spread that 'Portrait of Tuffy' about. If anyone was ever

going to hang what was left of it on the wall again, they'd have to give it a new name.

They'd have to call it 'Battle's End'. And guess who won?

Ellie picked up the frame with all the stringy bits hanging down. 'Tuffy!' she scolded as sternly as she could. 'Look what you've done to Mummy's very first painting! You've *destroyed* it.'

What a tragedy – I *don't* think. And if you want my opinion, they won't be howling with grief down at the Art Gallery, either, when they hear the news. Ellie's mother might be clever enough to bring a dead car back to life for long enough to drive to her art class and back, but she can't paint for toffee.

I can paint better than she can with my *paws*. And next time she leaves one of her nice new expensive blank white canvases about, I might just prove it to her.

Oh, yes. Indeed I might.

4: 'A riot of beauty'

SO WHITEWASH MY whiskers! I took a short cut over her precious new canvas. I was in a *hurry*. How was I to know she'd left it for only a minute while she went back in the house to look for her paintbrush?

There it was, lying on the patio, all nice and flat and neat and white and clean and – well, yes – *blank*.

Ready to go, you could say.

I expect I just wasn't *thinking* when I stepped in the tub of blue paint – by mistake – before running over the canvas to the gate.

26

And anyone could have been
clumsy enough to knock over that tub
of red paint when they ran back to

check out that smell of fish round the
dustbins.

How could it be my fault that one of

my paws slid in the tub of yellow before I took a swipe at that butterfly? How was I to know I was going to get paint droplets all over?

And you certainly can't blame me because my tail just happened to flick in the tub of green before I prowled round the ruined canvas a few times, dragging my tail behind me as I worried about the splatters.

Colourful, though. Cheerful. Rather fresh and 'modern'.

Mrs Famous-Artist-To-Be wasn't at all pleased. 'A brand-new canvas! Totally spoiled! Look at this mess! And I was planning to paint a lovely sunset on a lake under a hill of buttercups!'

Ellie stuck up for me. 'Tuffy wasn't being *bad*. He just got to the canvas first.'

I took a look at my handiwork. Ellie was right. Fancy a sunset? I had that

giant streak of red. You want a lake?
I had a splodge of blue. Buttercups?
Plenty of droplets of yellow in that
painting. On a hill? No worries. Tons
of green.

I gave Our Lady of the Paintbrush a

lofty stare. 'That's not a mess,' the look
said. 'That is proper *art*.'

And Ellie clearly thought so too. She
didn't dare say a word until Mrs Picasso
had driven off to her class. (Bang!
Rattle! X@%*%$! Phut! Cough!) But
then Ellie said to her father, 'I really like
it. Can we hang it on the wall?'

Usually, he'd have more tact. But he's
still mad at her ladyship for not taking
useful 'Fix Your Rubbish Heap Car'
lessons instead of art. And he hates
wasting anything, even a hook in a wall.
So he picked up the painting and hung
it up over the sofa.

Ellie stared at it with her hands
clasped in wonder. (You have to hand it
to that girl, she may be wet, wet, wet –
but she is loyal.)

'I'm going to call it "A Riot of
Beauty",' she said.

I turned a critical eye on my first-ever work of art.

Not sure about the 'Beauty' bit. But liked the 'Riot'.

Yes. Liked the 'Riot'.

5: *A droplet of advice*

SO MRS Watch-My-Fingers-Weave-Enchantment comes home that afternoon with three manky lumps of dried mud.

(I kid you not. Dried lumps of mud. If they'd been green, you would have thought of them as giant bogeys.)

'I didn't have a canvas,' she explained. (Frosty look at me – I just ignored it.) 'So I moved on to pottery.'

Pottery?

Potty, more like, if you want the opinion of that talented pussycat who painted 'A Riot of Beauty'.

I put my paw out to stroke one of
the lumps.

Accident! It fell to pieces before it
even hit the ground.

36

'Tuffy!' she said. 'How could you!
First you tread paint all over my lovely
clean canvas, and now you've broken
one of my pretty new pots.'

Pretty new pots? Puh-*lease*. They are

not pretty. The mud comes from a primeval swamp. And if you dropped so much as a pin into something that lumpy, you'd never find it again.

She put the other two pots safely up on the shelf. 'There!' she said. 'Not

even Tuffy can get up here and knock them off.'

A tiny droplet of advice: don't ever challenge a cat. It may have been a bit of an effort. (I don't keep as trim as I should.) But finally – finally – I managed to rise to the occasion and get up on that shelf.

Those pots up there were even worse than the one I'd knocked on to the floor. (By *accident*.) Talk about ugly! They had lumps hanging off here, and extra lumps sagging off there. One of them even had a kind of wart on its bottom, so every time I gave it a tiny little push, it wobbled horribly.

Uh-oh!

I'd like to tell you that it shattered into a thousand pieces. (That would sound good.) But it was such a lump of old rubbish it only fell into two halves.

Never mind. Be fair to me. At least the thing was *gone*.

Two down.

And one to go.

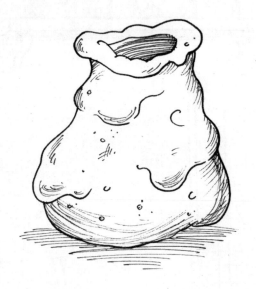

6: Little Miss Last Ugly Pot

I WASN'T THE only one in the house to hate those ugly pots enough to want to be rid of all of them. Next morning I strolled into the living room at my usual time to find Ellie's father sitting on the sofa, right next to my sunny spot.

There was a look in his eye I'd never seen before. For a moment I couldn't work out what it was, and then I realized he was pleased to see me.

Weird, or what?

He put out a welcoming hand. 'Come on, pussy. Here, pussy.'

Well, stretch my stripes! 'Come on,

43

pussy'? The man's never pined for my
company before. Do I recall many a
happy hour spent on his lap being
gently stroked and petted?

No, I do not.

Clearly he wanted something. I took a quick look round the room and –

Voila! He'd moved Little Miss Last Ugly Pot down to the coffee table. Aha! So that's what he was hoping for! An action replay of yesterday's excellent

result: one little soft paw out prodding, one quick cry of 'Whoops!', and a freshly smashed pot in the rubbish bin.

I won't say I wasn't tempted. That was one nasty pot. The world would be a prettier place for being rid of it. If I am scrupulously honest, I think that pot would have looked *nicer* in bits on the floor than it did as one lump on the table.

And I'm an obliging family pet, always keen to help out when I can.

I stuck my paw out, ready.

Then he made his big mistake.

'That's right,' he said. 'Good boy!'

Good boy? What does he think I am? A stupid *dog*?

I gave him the cool slow blink. If he'd had anything but cloth for brains, he would have known what it meant. That blink meant: Excuse me. Which of us is the one who's trained like a dog? Do I do what you want? No, I do not. Do I come when you call? No. I go my own sweet way. I am a *cat*.

You, on the other hand, are perfectly well trained. If I am hungry, all I have to do is walk round your legs a few times, half-tripping you, and you open a tin. If I want to go out, I stand by the door and yowl as if I'm about to throw up, and you're over in a flash to open it.

Who is the one who should be saying, 'Good boy!' round here, Buster?

Yes. Not you. *Me*.

More than one way to make a point, of course. I chose to do it by giving him the runaround. I kept him on tenterhooks, padding up and down the coffee table. (He is such a *hypocrite*. Usually he'd push me off.) I let my fur graze the pot more closely every time I passed, and every now and again I even stretched out a paw as if to stroke that nasty pottery lump he was so hoping I would break.

I even gave it a little push so it toppled a little.

Almost fell off the side.

Almost.

Not quite.

'Come *on*,' he urged me. 'You can do it. You're a clumsy enough cat.'

Clumsy, eh? So things were getting

nasty. I could have told him: not a thing gets smashed by me in this house unless I choose to smash it. Call us cats clever. Call us cunning. Call us caterwauling.

But *never* call us clumsy.

And then he really blew it. He changed tack.

'Come on,' he wheedled. 'Smash it for me. *Please*. Sweet pussy. Sweet, sweet pussy.'

How *dare* he! What a nerve! Can you *believe* this man? Five years we've lived together, and he calls me 'sweet'.

It is an *insult*.

I felt like scratching him, I really did. Instead, I took revenge. I made my eyes go huge, and sent my fur up on end. I did my 'Just-Seen-a-Ghost-in-the-Doorway' act. (It's *very* good.) And then, to put the icing on the cake, I shot backwards along the coffee table

at about a hundred miles an hour until
I'd knocked the pretty china dish he
loves so much off at the other end,
shattering it to pieces and spilling all

the coins he keeps in there on to the floor.

He was still chasing money round the room when the doorbell rang.

Mr Harris from next door. And, as usual, he was selling raffle tickets.

'Sorry,' said Ellie's father as he always did. 'Unfortunately, just at this moment I happen to be out of spare change.'

Mr Harris looked at the money spilling out of Ellie's father's cupped hands.

'All that will do,' he said. 'All that will buy at least one ticket. And it's a really good prize – especially for your family. It's a brand-new car.'

(Clearly we cats are not the only ones round here who are fed up with coughing for an hour or two each time anyone in my family sets off on a car trip.)

So what could Ellie's father do? He

had to buy a ticket or look the cheapskate he is. By the time he came back, he was in a real temper.

I find unpleasantness in others a terrible trial. We cats do have our dignity. All that I chose to do was push

the last ugly pot well away from the table edge. I shifted it this way a bit. Then I shifted it that. And then I left it sitting very safely indeed, right in the middle, where no one could ever knock it over and break it by mistake.

Then I stuck my tail up, proudly high, and I stalked out.

7: Cat and mouse

SO THEN WE ended up playing a sort
of Cat and Mouse game. (Guess who
played Mouse!) He put the ugly pot
back on the shelf in case The Budding
Artist got suspicious. But he still wanted
it gone, and to be able to spread his
hands – Mr All Innocence – and swear
to Ellie's mother that it was I who
broke it.

Over the next few weeks, he must
have tried everything. And I mean
everything.

First, he tried wheedling and
begging. You know the sort of stuff.

'Dear pussy. Kind pussy. Won't you do one tiny eensy-weensy thing for me?'

(Well, as my old granny used to say, 'Please pass the sick bag, Alice!')

56

Then he tried picking me up and putting me on the shelf and pushing me along it.

That's right. Actually putting his

hand on my bottom and trying to *push* me. (He's still nursing the scratches from that one.)

After that, he smeared whipping

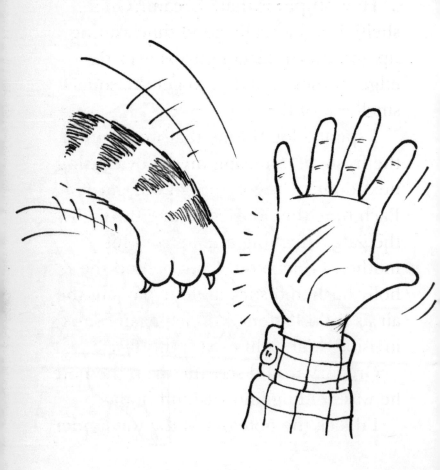

cream on the pot, hoping that I'd be greedy enough to jump up and lick the pot so hard it would move along the shelf and fall off the end.

How stupid is that? Cream? On a shelf? I had a really good time skating up and down, kicking drips over the edge. It took him *days* to get the sour smell out of the rugs.

I spent a lot of time that week out in the fresh air, amusing myself by chasing next door's Gregory out of our garden. Each time the poor boy came through the gate, clutching a note from his mother, I'd leap out from behind the holly bush and stick all four paws in the air as if I'd flattened myself against an invisible wall right next to his face.

Gregory would scream, drop the note he was holding and rush off home.

I'd kick the note out of the way under

the holly bush (hiding the evidence) and go back to sleep on the wall.

A stupid game, maybe. But I enjoyed it and it passed the time until Ellie's father had spent enough time scrubbing the rugs to make the living room smell pleasant again. Then I came back inside, to find my adversary in the War of the Last Ugly Pot getting even more cunning.

He'd dropped a fine fresh prawn inside the thing.

'There!' he crowed. 'Try to resist that, Tuffy! Try to get that out without knocking the pot over the edge!'

Well, I was tempted. If there's one thing that I love, it's a fresh prawn. But then I thought, nobody, not even a mothwallet like Ellie's father, has the nerve to buy only one. There must be others!

I went off to the toolshed and found the rest of them still in the bag, hidden from Ellie's mother, waiting for the secret little luxury snack he was planning for himself later.

Things worked out nicely. I ate those instead.

8: Before six o'clock tonight

ON MY WAY back through the garden,
Bella and Tiger and Pusskins yowled
at me from the wall where they were
sitting watching Ellie's mother trying
to park.

'That car of your family's!' said Bella.
'It's a real *disgrace*.'

'Pouring out smoke,' agreed Pusskins.

Tiger was even more grumpy. 'We
could all choke to *death*.' He was still
moaning as Ellie's mother came up the
path with her most recent triumph.
'And what is *that*? A heap of knitted
twigs?'

64

'That's her new work of art,' I had to admit. 'She's given up on pottery and moved on to "garden sculptures".'

'Those manky old bits of trailing raffia are going to get *everywhere*,' grumbled Bella. 'And is that a flag on the top? Or did some lavatory paper get stuck to whatever it is on the way home?'

Ellie's mother staggered through the gate and dumped her new great work of art on to the lawn. Smoke was still

pouring out of the car, but she didn't notice. She was waving at Ellie.

'Come and see my new piece. I'm calling it "Wigwam in Summer"!'

Ellie came rushing over, clasping her hands. 'Oooh!' she cried. 'It's lovely. It's beautiful! Can I have it as my own little house? Then I can sit inside it and play Let's Pretend!'

Tiger just rolled his eyes and Bella pretended kindly that she hadn't heard. I mean, everyone's embarrassed by their family. That is the Way of the World. But Ellie is more than a few steps beyond soft. She has become Essence of Mush.

But all that 'sitting inside it' talk had given Bella an idea.

'Excellent loo for cats, that wigwam,' she couldn't help observing. 'Just the right size. Very private. And you could

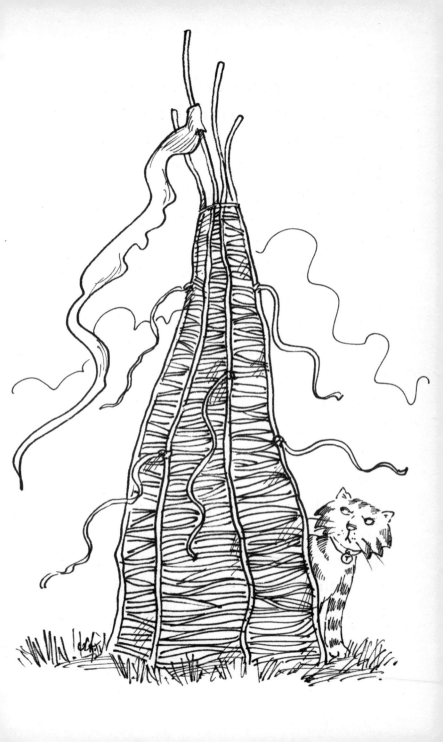

fly that loo paper flag on top to let people know whenever it's in use.'

'And *how* it's in use,' added Tiger. He turned to me. 'That's Symbolism, that is,' he explained. 'I know because someone in my family took the Great Books course at that very same college.'

'Let's hope she moves the wigwam on to a flowerbed,' said Pusskins. 'That'll make for easier scratching in after.'

I do live in a family. 'Hey, fellas!' I rebuked them. 'What about poor Ellie? She won't want to sit and play Let's Pretend in a public lavatory.'

We were still arguing when the car that had been sitting there busily puffing out smoke suddenly burst into flames. It was a good show, what with the fire engines. ('*Nee-naw! Nee-naw!*' We'll all be practising that noise on the prowl tonight.) And at the end, Bella said, 'A pity Ellie's father can't find that winning raffle ticket of his, and get his new car.'

'Sorry?' I said.

She turned my way. 'Didn't you know? The raffle draw was a whole week ago. According to the book of ticket stubs, Ellie's dad has the winning number. But Mr Harris says that, according to the rules, the winner has to show up with the ticket to claim the prize.'

'Before six o'clock,' added Pusskins. 'This evening. On the dot. Otherwise the new car goes to the runner-up.'

'All this is news to me,' I said, a shade uneasily.

'I can't think why,' said Tiger. 'Everyone else knows. And Ellie's mother and father must know as well because Mr Harris has sent Gregory round at least a dozen times with notes to tell them.'

I felt even more uneasy. Glancing
guiltily towards the litter gathered
under the holly bush, I couldn't help
muttering, 'Dear me. Oh, dear me.
Oh, dear.'

'I expect the raffle ticket's been lost,' said Pusskins. 'Those things are very light and small. It must be terribly easy for everyone in the household to forget where they put it.'

I found myself staring at a cloud sailing over my head, and saying nothing.

Everyone round me sighed.

'We'd all have a better life if your family had a new car,' said Bella. 'They would go off on more day trips. Leave us to ourselves a bit.'

We all fell silent, thinking of the good times we used to have racing around the living room, ripping up the cushions and scaring the goldfish silly.

'Oh, all *right*!' I said.

Take it from me, it is *no joke*, sticking your head in a holly bush. I had to stretch really far to find a note that wasn't badly ripped. Bella's a tubby tabby, so she helped me roll it flat. (We quite enjoyed that idle hour on the warm flagstones.)

And then I slid it under the back door.

It was Ellie's mother who picked it up, of course. 'George! George! We've won a car! In a raffle! All that we have to do is find the ticket you bought from Gregory's dad, and the car will be ours!' She rushed towards him. 'So where did you put it to keep it safe?'

She skidded to a halt. 'George?' she said. 'George? You do remember where you put it, don't you?'

Ellie and I turned round to look at him.

He had gone green.

9: 'Run, Daddy! Run!'

OF COURSE, THE poor sap hadn't got a clue. I watched them turn the house upside down, up-ending sofas, peering under rugs, sticking their noses into old envelopes.

By the time the clock ticked round to a quarter to six, they were quite desperate.

'It must be *somewhere*!'

'Where did you put it? Try to remember!'

He clutched his hair and wailed, 'I don't know! All I can recall is coming back into this room with the raffle ticket in my hand.'

I tried to give them a hint. I kept on strolling up and down along the shelf, and giving little purrs. But they had no time to pay attention to me.

So, in the end, with only five minutes to go before the deadline, I had to do what he'd been trying to get me to do for several weeks.

I didn't *choose* to do it, you understand. It was an Unselfish Act, purely for the Good of the Community. Left to myself, I would have happily broken my own front left leg rather

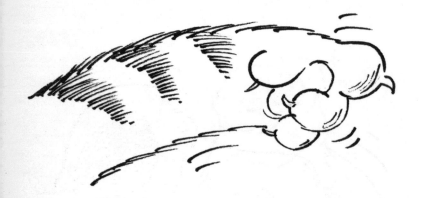

than please him by damaging that last ugly pot.

But needs must when the devil drives. I stuck out my paw and pushed the thing firmly off the end of the shelf.

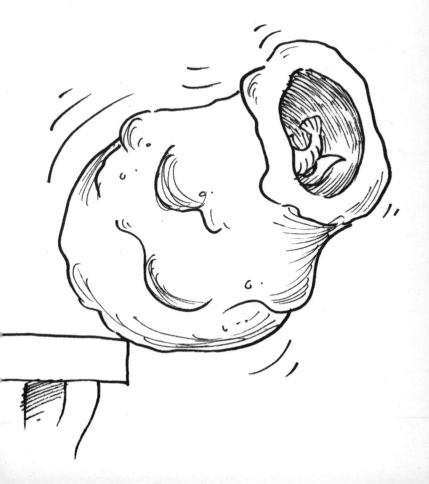

I won't say it smashed. Fat chance.
This pot was such an ill-made lump, it
simply fell apart in mid-air.

Out tumbled, first, one fresh prawn,
then one small raffle ticket.

The bits of pot hit the carpet. Blop!
Blop! Blop!

'What on *earth* is that prawn doing
there?' said Ellie's mother.

He didn't take the time to blush. He
simply snatched up the raffle ticket and
made for the door.

'Run, Daddy! Run!' cried Ellie.

10: A moral victory and
a good result

THE GANG TOLD me all about it afterwards.

'Didn't go round by the pavement. Simply jumped over the fence.'

'Amazing! No doubt about it, it was an Olympic-standard leap.'

'He practically bust his truss doing it.'

I was sorry to have missed the show. But I was too busy being cuddled and praised by sweet little Ellie. 'Oh, Tuffy! You're the cleverest, most wonderful cat in the whole wide world. You found the ticket! Just in time. And now we're

going to have a brand-new car. I love you, Tuffy. I love you. You're a sweetie, peetie, weetie –'

Okay, okay! Enough! I can't take too much of the soppy stuff. I shook her off

and I went out. I wanted to be alone. I had a thing or two to think about up on my wall. After all, I'd had to make a giant sacrifice. I'd had to do what Ellie's father wanted all along, and break the pot.

I hate doing things for that man.
Normally I'd rather tear off my own left
ear than try to please him. But it was
for the best. Bella was right. Now they
had a better car, they'd go out a whole
lot more. I might have lost the battle,

but at least, in doing so, I had won the battleground.

It was an honourable defeat.

A moral victory and a good result.